Busy! Busy! Busy!

Jonathan Shipton was born in Birmingham in 1948. He attended Leicester University and worked as a retail jeweller before moving to a smallholding in Wales in 1973. Jonathan still lives in Wales today at Llanwrda, Dyfed.

Also available by Jonathan Shipton is *In the Night*, illustrated by Gill Scriven, published in hardback by Collins

Born in Suffolk in 1938, Michael Foreman studied art at Lowestoft and London. He has worked as an art director on several magazines and has made six animated films for the BBC. Michael is the illustrator of over seventy books and author of twenty, and has twice won both the Kate Greenaway award and the Francis Williams Prize. He is married with three children and divides his time between London and St Ives. Michael Foreman's illustrations can also be found in *Fairytales of Gold* by Alan Garner, published in hardback by Collins

First published in Great Britain by Andersen Press Ltd in 1991
First published in Picture Lions in 1993
Picture Lions is an imprint of the Children's Division,
part of HarperCollins Publishers Limited,
77-85 Fulham Palace Road, Hammersmith,
London W6 8JB

Printed in Great Britain

Busy! Busy! Busy!

Story by
JONATHAN SHIPTON
Illustrated by
MICHAEL FOREMAN

PictureLions
An Imprint of HarperCollins*Publishers*

One fine day
Mum was in a bad mood.
She wouldn't give me a biscuit,
or read me a story,
or play,
or anything.

Mum said,
there was too much to do.
She had beds to make and
meals to cook and
clothes to wash.

She said she was chained to the kitchen sink all day! She said I had

to go away and play by myself. So I did!

I went upstairs and sorted out the farm and

I tidied up the cars and I even found a long lost sock.

But all the while down below I could still hear Mum

crashing around with her bad mood. Then suddenly . . .

. . . the whole house went quiet. I held my breath.

I listened really hard. But I couldn't hear a thing.

So I tip-toed downstairs to see what was going on.

The kitchen door was open a tiny crack. I peeped inside.

There she was. Standing very still. With hands stuck in

the sink and two big tears rolling down her cheeks.

In a flash I was onto the chair.

And I wiped away the tears.

And I gave her a Great Big Kiss.

Then I pulled her arms from the water and shouted,
"SNIP! SNIP! SNIP!" to the chains around the sink, and they all
fell off like magic.

"Come on Mum," I said. "Quick, before it's too late." So we grabbed hands and we ran down the corridor into the sunshine.

Just the two of us.

Just in time.

Here are some more Picture Lions

for you to enjoy